A Note to Parents and Caregivers:

Read-it! Readers are for children who are just starting on the amazing road to reading. These beautiful books support both the acquisition of reading skills and the love of books.

 The PURPLE LEVEL presents basic topics and objects using high frequency words and simple language patterns.

 The RED LEVEL presents familiar topics using common words and repeating sentence patterns.

 The BLUE LEVEL presents new ideas using a larger vocabulary and varied sentence structure.

 The YELLOW LEVEL presents more challenging ideas, a broad vocabulary, and wide variety in sentence structure.

 The GREEN LEVEL presents more complex ideas, an extended vocabulary range, and expanded language structures.

 The ORANGE LEVEL presents a wide range of ideas and concepts using challenging vocabulary and complex language structures.

When sharing a book with your child, read in short stretches, pausing often to talk about the pictures. Have your child turn the pages and point to the pictures and familiar words. And be sure to reread favorite stories or parts of stories.

There is no right or wrong way to share books with children. Find time to read with your child, and pass on the legacy of literacy.

Adria F. Klein, Ph.D.
Professor Emeritus
California State University
San Bernardino, California

Editor: Jill Kalz
Designer: Abbey Fitzgerald
Page Production: Michelle Biedscheid
Art Director: Nathan Gassman
Associate Managing Editor: Christianne Jones
The illustrations in this book were created digitally.

Picture Window Books
5115 Excelsior Boulevard
Suite 232
Minneapolis, MN 55416
877-845-8392
www.picturewindowbooks.com

Printed in the United States of America.

Library of Congress Cataloging-in-Publication Data
Redmond, Shirley-Raye, 1955-
Pup's prairie home / by Shirley Raye Redmond ; illustrated by Matthew Skeens.
p. cm. — (Read-it! readers)
ISBN-13: 978-1-4048-4084-3 (library binding)
[1. Prairie dogs—Fiction. 2. Animals—Infancy—Fiction.] I. Skeens, Matthew, ill.
II. Title.
PZ7.R24548Pu 2008
[E]—dc22   2007032912

Pup's Prairie Home

by Shirley Raye Redmond
illustrated by Matthew Skeens

Special thanks to our reading adviser:

Adria F. Klein, Ph.D.
Professor Emeritus, California State University
San Bernardino, California

PICTURE WINDOW BOOKS
Minneapolis, Minnesota

Pup and his mom lived in a prairie dog town.

Their home was a deep, dark hole in the ground.

One day, Pup saw a different kind of town. He saw tall houses and short houses.

He saw yellow houses, blue houses, and other houses, too.

"I want to live in a house!" Pup cried.

"A deep, dark hole is the best home for a prairie dog pup like you," his mom said.

The next day, Pup saw a playground.
He saw two swings and a long slide.

He saw a merry-go-round and a sandbox, too.

"I want to live on a playground!"
Pup cried.

"A deep, dark hole is the best home for a prairie dog pup like you," his mom said.

Then Pup saw a garden.

He saw tomatoes, corn, and pumpkins.
He saw carrots and watermelon, too.

"I want to live in a garden!" Pup cried.

"A deep, dark hole is the best home for a prairie dog pup like you," his mom said.

Just then, Pup heard a screech. He looked up. It was a hungry hawk!

Pup's mom saw the hawk, too.
"Danger, Pup!" she cried. "Run
home! Run as fast as you can!"

The hawk swooped down. Pup and his mom dived into their hole. The other prairie dogs dived into their holes, too.

The hawk screeched again. Then it gave up and flew away. The prairie dog town was safe.

Pup felt sleepy. It was time for his nap. "Mom, I don't want to live anywhere else," he said.

"A deep, dark hole is the best home for a prairie dog pup like me."

More *Read-it!* Readers

Bright pictures and fun stories help you practice your reading skills. Look for more books at your level.

Bears on Ice
The Bossy Rooster
The Camping Scare
Dust Bunnies
Emily's Pictures
Flying with Oliver
Frog Pajama Party
Galen's Camera
Greg Gets a Hint
The Kickball Game

Last in Line
The Lifeguard
Mike's Night-light
Nate the Dinosaur
One Up for Brad
Robin's New Glasses
The Sassy Monkey
The Treasure Map
Tuckerbean
What's Bugging Pamela?

On the Web

FactHound offers a safe, fun way to find Web sites related to topics in this book. All of the sites on FactHound have been researched by our staff.

1. Visit *www.facthound.com*

2. Type in this special code:
   1404840842

3. Click on the FETCH IT button.

Your trusty FactHound will fetch the best sites for you!
A complete list of *Read-it!* Readers is available on our Web site:
www.picturewindowbooks.com